Bold Words from Black Men

For my dear old dad, Ballard Dean McPherson;
my elegant, kind, and funny granddad, Willie Ross;
my sons, Noah, Milo, and Zen;
all the ancestors I can and cannot name;
and this book's editor, Denene Millner, for doing the work
and inspiring me to do more Bold Words.
—T. P.

To my mother, who's been with me every step of my artistic journey,
allowing and supporting me—thank you. I extend my heartfelt appreciation to all artists
around the world who generously share their wisdom with aspiring peers without exclusion.
To all visual artists, this book is for you. May it inspire you to embrace your creativity
and paint your unique stories on the canvas of the world. May we continue to inspire,
share knowledge, and support one another, for in each other lies our strength.
With gratitude and love.
—D. C. N.

SIMON & SCHUSTER BOOKS FOR YOUNG READERS
An imprint of Simon & Schuster Children's Publishing Division
1230 Avenue of the Americas, New York, New York 10020
Text © 2025 by Tamara Pizzoli
Illustration © 2025 by Desire Cesar Ngabo
Book design by Alicia Mikles
All rights reserved, including the right of reproduction in whole or in part in any form.
SIMON & SCHUSTER BOOKS FOR YOUNG READERS and related marks are trademarks of Simon & Schuster, LLC.
For information about special discounts for bulk purchases, please contact Simon & Schuster Special Sales at 1-866-506-1949 or business@simonandschuster.com.
The Simon & Schuster Speakers Bureau can bring authors to your live event. For more information or to book an event, contact the
Simon & Schuster Speakers Bureau at 1-866-248-3049 or visit our website at www.simonspeakers.com.
The text for this book was set in Aachen Pro, Ayr Blufy, Franklin Gothic, Memphis, Montecatini Pro, and The Pretender.
The illustrations for this book were rendered digitally.
Manufactured in China
1224 SCP
First Edition
2 4 6 8 10 9 7 5 3 1
CIP data for this book is available from the Library of Congress.
ISBN 9781665930642
ISBN 9781665930659 (ebook)

BOLD WORDS FROM BLACK MEN

Insights and Reflections from 50 Notable Trailblazers Who Influenced the World

CURATED BY DR. TAMARA PIZZOLI

ILLUSTRATED BY DESIRE CESAR "EL'CESART" NGABO

A DENENE MILLNER BOOK
SIMON & SCHUSTER BOOKS FOR YOUNG READERS
NEW YORK LONDON TORONTO SYDNEY NEW DELHI

CONTENTS

Introduction	vii		
Ermias Joseph Asghedom (aka Nipsey Hussle)	2	Malcolm X	52
Michael Jackson	4	Prince Rogers Nelson	54
Martin Luther King Jr.	6	Chadwick Aaron Boseman	56
Kendrick Lamar	8	Olivier Rousteing	58
Quincy Jones	10	Frederick August Kittel Jr. (aka August Wilson)	60
Sidney Poitier	12	Jean-Michel Basquiat	62
Kevin Hart	14	James Arthur Baldwin	64
Eddie Murphy	16	Colin Kaepernick	66
Jermaine Lamarr Cole (aka J. Cole)	18	Robert "Bob" Nesta Marley	68
Nasir bin Olu Dara Jones (aka Nas)	20	Alvin Ailey Jr.	70
Colin Powell	22	Gil Scott-Heron	72
Tyler Perry	24	John Lewis	74
Iddris Sandu	26	Cory Booker	76
Neil deGrasse Tyson	28	Thurgood Marshall	78
Marcus Samuelsson	30	Gordon Parks	80
Derrick Jones (aka D-Nice)	32	Denzel Washington	82
Sir Lewis Hamilton	34	Jesse Williams	84
Trevor Noah	36	Shelton Jackson "Spike" Lee	86
Nelson Mandela	38	Jesse Owens	88
André Lauren Benjamin (aka André 3000)	40	Savion Glover	90
Myles Frost	42	Jackie Robinson	92
Ahmir Thompson (aka Questlove)	44	Sean Anderson (aka Big Sean)	94
Virgil Abloh	46	Ryan Coogler	96
Barack Hussein Obama	48	Shawn Carter (aka Jay-Z)	98
Kehinde Wiley	50	LeBron James	100

INTRODUCTION

In 2022, my book *Bold Words from Black Women* was published and released into the world. I waited, as so many authors do, to witness the feedback and verdict from readers. In retrospect, I'm not certain that I was expecting as much as I was knowing that most readers would find themselves completely smitten with that gorgeous book. As the reviews began rolling in, I smiled for days, knowing that the book you now hold would soon be on the way.

I began collecting quotes for *Bold Words from Black Men* long before Denene Millner formally committed to publishing it. Over several months, the wise words from Black men of varied backgrounds and experiences seemed to find me. I'd come across a powerful quote while watching a cooking show, listening to a podcast, or flipping through the pages of a magazine, and then boom—a gem worth listening to, applying, and sharing would emerge. I'd scramble to grab a pen and paper to catch the jewel that had just been dropped, knowing that eventually it could make its way to a page in this book.

Curating quotes for *Bold Words from Black Men* differed greatly from the approach I used to select the content for *Bold Words from Black Women*. I am the mother of four children: Noah, Milo, Zen, and Lotus. Noah, my eldest son, is a fresh thirteen at the time of this writing. This year has been a very unique and challenging one for him. In fact, it has been a transformative year for us both. While Noah officially became a teenager this past spring, for the first time, I have begun to understand what it means to mother a child who I will always see as my baby but who is viewed as a young Black man by so many others. Choosing the right words to help him navigate this tricky terrain felt urgent. Personal.

I chose these quotes with transitions in mind, those that await us all again and again in life, but particularly those that young Black boys and men experience. With them on my heart, I searched for words of affirmation, power, resilience, truth, beauty, love, whimsy, wonder, success, faith, spirit, and purpose spoken by Black men who are not perfect—and don't have to be—but have a true impact. The lived Black experience at any age is a distinct one, and though the men included in this book are of varied shades of brown, it is important to emphasize that this book is for everyone to engage with and enjoy.

There's no manual or road map to navigate the journey of what the late musical virtuoso Prince once referred to as "this thing called life." I do believe that it is a genuine gift in our human experience to receive a kind word, nudge, nugget of advice, anecdote, or bit of perspective from someone who has done and learned a great deal. In a podcast I recently enjoyed, the rapper Big Sean intimated that how we get through life and what we make of our time here depend on our technique, and technique is something that can and should be developed, practiced, studied, and, if necessary, changed. It is something that, like us, can evolve. That concept deeply impacted me, and I find it applicable to my goal for this book. It is my hope, dear reader, that you find something—many things—of value and use within these pages, words that assist you in the ongoing development of your very own unique and splendid life technique.

BOLD WORDS FROM BLACK MEN

> "MASTER YOUR ENERGY.
> DO YOUR BEST TO MASTER
> YOUR ENERGY AND
> WHAT YOU PUT OUT."

ERMIAS JOSEPH ASGHEDOM (AKA NIPSEY HUSSLE)

Rapper. Entrepreneur.
(August 15, 1985–March 31, 2019)

In a 2018 interview with 247HH, the rapper discussed the importance of being aware that everything one puts out into the world returns in a different form. He encouraged listeners to adjust their words, thoughts, and actions to yield a better day-to-day reality.

> "THAT'S WHAT GOD
> GAVE US TALENT FOR...
> TO HELP PEOPLE AND
> TO GIVE BACK."

MICHAEL JACKSON

**King of Pop. Singer. Dancer. Songwriter.
(August 29, 1958–June 25, 2009)**

In a 2005 interview in which he talked about his love for dancing, music, and performing, Michael Jackson, a global pop icon who is considered one of the most important cultural figures of the twentieth century, explained that talent expressed through art can be shared with others in tangible ways that have a real-world impact.

"What is in your life's blueprint? . . .
What you do now and what you decide now at this age
may well determine which way your life shall go.
And whenever a building is constructed, you usually have
an architect who draws a blueprint, and that blueprint
serves as the pattern, as the guide, as the model
for those who are to build a building. . . .
Now each of you is in the process of building
the structure of your lives, and the question is whether you
have a proper, a solid, and a sound blueprint."

MARTIN LUTHER KING JR.

Minister. Activist. Civil rights leader.
(January 15, 1929–April 4, 1968)

In 1967, Dr. King gave a short but powerful speech to the students of Barratt Junior High School in Philadelphia, highlighting that the choices the students made at that point in their lives could very well impact their entire life's path. He emphasized the importance of having a deep belief in one's own dignity and worth, the beauty of being Black with Black features, being determined to achieve excellence, studying hard and staying in school, and being ready to walk through doors of opportunity.

"SPEAK ON SELF;
REFLECTION OF SELF FIRST.
THAT'S WHERE THE INITIAL CHANGE
WILL START FROM."

KENDRICK LAMAR

Rapper. Producer. Songwriter.
(June 17, 1987–)

In a 2017 interview with *Rolling Stone*, Kendrick Lamar was asked why he had not spoken about the forty-fifth president of the United States, who was in office at the time. Lamar replied that instead of simply talking, we should take action and that he had personally committed to work in his own community to enact real change.

"IF YOU KNOW WHERE YOU COME FROM, IT MAKES IT EASIER FOR YOU TO GET WHERE YOU'RE GOING. AND YOU HAVE TO ACCEPT THAT. I WAS ALWAYS HAPPY TO TALK TO MY ELDERS AND LEARN LESSONS."

QUINCY JONES

(March 14, 1933–)
Arranger. Composer. Producer.

In an interview with Qwest TV, Quincy Jones discussed the connection between culture and music and how the elements of dance found in Black hip-hop culture can be traced to West Africa and Brazil. He stressed the importance of knowing your history so that your future path is clearer.

"OF ALL MY FATHER'S TEACHINGS, THE MOST ENDURING WAS THE ONE ABOUT THE TRUE MEASURE OF A MAN. THAT TRUE MEASURE WAS HOW WELL HE PROVIDED FOR HIS CHILDREN, AND IT STUCK WITH ME AS IF IT WERE ETCHED IN MY BRAIN."

SIDNEY POITIER

Actor. Director. Diplomat.
(February 20, 1927–January 6, 2022)

In his 2000 autobiography, *The Measure of a Man: A Spiritual Autobiography*, the celebrated actor reflected on the many life lessons he'd learned throughout his years. The most significant, he said, came from his father, who taught him about the importance of fathers providing well for their children.

"There is no ceiling to success. There's no limit. . . . For me, it's about creating opportunities for . . . the generation behind me. My star is bright; it's not going to get brighter, but if I can help create the opportunities for others, then I'm happy."

KEVIN HART

Comedian. Actor. Producer.
(July 6, 1979–)

In a 2021 interview, Kevin Hart discussed the satisfaction he gains from sharing his show business knowledge with the Black community and creating opportunities for Black creatives and future executives. Achieving a high level of success, he added, has allowed him to produce projects that interest him while creating a blueprint for up-and-coming talent.

"POSITIVITY, CREATIVITY, FORWARD MOTION. THOSE THREE THINGS PRETTY MUCH COVER EVERYTHING. WHENEVER THINGS GET CRAZY, IF YOU GO BACK TO THAT, YOU GET GROUNDED."

EDDIE MURPHY

Actor. Comedian. Producer. Singer. Writer.
(April 3, 1961–)

While reflecting on a remarkable career that has earned him an Oscar nomination and an Emmy Award, Murphy offered these key words that describe the guiding force that helped him succeed and continues to drive his future.

"WHEN YOU PUT YOURSELF IN UNCOMFORTABLE MOMENTS, YOU FIND OUT A LOT ABOUT YOURSELF. AND USUALLY, YOU FIND OUT THAT YOU'RE CAPABLE OF RISING TO THAT BAR THAT'S SET BY THAT UNCOMFORTABLE SITUATION."

JERMAINE LAMARR COLE (AKA J. COLE)

Rapper. Songwriter. Producer.
(January 28, 1985–)

In a documentary covering his album *The Off-Season*, J. Cole talked about the importance of striving for excellence, even when you've achieved and surpassed your initial goals. Success, he explained, breeds comfort and can stifle creativity. Raising the bar for your personal best, even once you begin achieving your goals, ensures excellence that endures.

"You don't want to miss going from zero to sixty. You don't want to miss the dash in between. That's a good time right there. It might be a little scary; it might be a little nervous at times. But . . . once you make it . . . you appreciate the struggling times. And if you just go from point A to Z like that, there's nowhere else to go."

NASIR BIN OLU DARA JONES (AKA NAS)

Rapper. Entrepreneur. Executive.
(September 14, 1973–)

In a 2013 interview about the state of hip-hop, this rap legend advised young creatives to resist racing to the heights of success, to instead savor each moment along the way, adding that even the difficult times are significant.

"Never neglect details,
even to the point of being a pest.
Moments of stress, confusion, and fatigue
are exactly when mistakes happen.
And when everyone else's mind
is dulled or distracted the leaders
must be doubly vigilant.
'Always check small things.'"

COLIN POWELL

Four-star general. First African-American secretary of state. Diplomat. Author.
(April 5, 1937–October 18, 2021)

In his 1995 autobiography, *My American Journey*, Colin Powell repeatedly highlights the importance of paying attention to every part of a project—even the smallest details—as it is essential to help leaders accomplish missions with maximum safety and success.

"I've never had an open door,
or an invitation or opportunity,
while I watched my white brothers
and sisters get opportunity after
opportunity, no matter if their shows
or movies fail or not. I understand
that this is the hand that I was dealt.
This Black skin . . . is beautiful.
I'm not going to apologize for it.
I'm not going to be ashamed of it.
But I'm going to make it work
for me and for us."

TYLER PERRY

Actor. Director. Producer. Screenwriter.
(September 13, 1969–)

In a 2020 interview, Tyler Perry shared that though the odds for success were stacked against him, he powered through a difficult childhood, many failures and setbacks, and even a stint being unhoused to attain the first of many career successes. He quickly realized that achieving his goals largely depended on him creating opportunities for himself and others while maintaining relentless belief in both his vision and his race as powerful assets.

"WHO'S TO SAY THAT THE NEXT MAJOR INNOVATION IN ARTIFICIAL INTELLIGENCE OR VOLUMETRIC CAPTURING OR SPATIAL REALITY CAN'T COME FROM BOYLE HEIGHTS, OR CAN'T COME FROM COMPTON, OR CAN'T COME FROM ATLANTA?"

IDDRIS SANDU

Architectural technologist.

(May 7, 1997–)

While he enjoys collaborating with notable brands and political groups, Iddris Sandu said in a 2020 interview that the biggest impact comes from empowering the next generation in underserved communities. He emphasized that the future of modern technology is ripe for innovation that begins in Black and brown minds and environments.

"Skill set goes obsolete every three or four years. You want to be trained in how to think and how to learn. You need the pliability and flexibility of encountering new ideas, and if you are turned off by new ideas, the world will leave you behind."

NEIL DEGRASSE TYSON

Astrophysicist. Author. Scientist.
(October 5, 1958–)

When asked to list the skills young people should have in today's job market, Tyson insisted in a 2021 interview that being an innovative, big thinker willing to learn is paramount to keeping up in a fast-paced, ever-evolving world.

> "YOU CAN'T COME IN AND TAKE ALL THE BENEFITS AND THEN, WHEN IT COMES YOUR TURN TO CHIP IN, LEAVE."

MARCUS SAMUELSSON

Chef. Author. Restaurateur.
(January 25, 1971–)

Marcus Samuelsson, an Ethiopia-born, Sweden-raised adoptee who found great success in the culinary world after immigrating to the United States, shared in a 2020 interview on NPR that because he personally and professionally benefited from the civil rights movement, he felt compelled to offer meals to neighborhoods economically devastated by the COVID-19 pandemic. While many chose to leave large cities, Samuelsson embraced the opportunity to give back to a community and country that had given him so much.

"DANCE WITH YOUR DAUGHTER, YOUR FATHER, YOUR SPOUSE. CELEBRATE EACH OTHER. WHEN YOU GO TO BED, I WANT YOU TO GO TO BED HAPPY AND JUST EXCITED FOR LIFE, BECAUSE LIFE IS SO PRECIOUS."

DERRICK JONES (AKA D-NICE)

DJ. Rapper. Producer.
(June 19, 1970–)

In a 2020 magazine interview, D-Nice explained how his decision to play select songs on Instagram Live following the onset of the global pandemic and resulting quarantine helped him and people all over the world cope with unprecedented isolation. Eventually dubbed "Club Quarantine," D-Nice's virtual DJ sets brought citizens and celebrities together to dance, reminisce, enjoy, and connect, despite the distance.

"I THINK IN ToDAY'S WORLD, YOU HAVE To TRANSCEND. YOU HAVE TO DO SOMETHING DIFFERENT. YOU HAVE TO SHOW YOUR UNIQUENESS AND NoT SHY AWAY FROM THAT."

SIR LEWIS HAMILTON

(January 7, 1985–)
Racing driver. Formula 1 world champion.

In a 2018 interview, Lewis Hamilton discussed the importance of maintaining his own identity while dominating and excelling in the field of professional race car driving, especially being the only Black competitor on the track. As the most successful Formula 1 driver in history, Hamilton often integrates his culture, love for hip-hop, activism, and entrepreneurship into his professional life.

"We spend so much time being afraid of failure, afraid of rejection. But regret is the thing we should fear most. Failure is an answer. Rejection is an answer. Regret is an eternal question you will never have the answer to."

TREVOR NOAH

Television host. Actor. Comedian. Political commentator.
(February 20, 1984–)

In his comedic autobiography, *Born a Crime: Stories from a South African Childhood*, Trevor Noah shares personal stories about growing up as the mixed-race son of a Black mother and a white father during apartheid in South Africa. In this passage, he advocates for taking chances even if doing so leads to disappointment, because it's better to have experiences than to be left wondering what could have been if one had simply tried.

"No one is born hating another person because of the colour of his skin, or his background, or his religion. People must learn to hate, and if they can learn to hate, they can be taught to love, for love comes more naturally to the human heart than its opposite."

NELSON MANDELA

(July 18, 1918–December 5, 2013)
First president of post-apartheid South Africa. Anti-apartheid revolutionary. Political leader.

In his 1994 autobiography entitled *Long Walk to Freedom*, Nelson Mandela covers lessons he learned throughout his childhood, his formative schooling years, and while incarcerated as an adult. As the principal leader of the movement that ultimately overthrew the unjust apartheid regime in South Africa, Mandela often underlined the value of love in restoring the natural equilibrium and the respect that humans have for one another at birth but sometimes lose through harmful conditioning.

"You got to put the time in to figure out who you are and what you not, too. . . . That's when your skin starts to breathe and you start to get into your primal self. And your primal self is the best contribution to the planet."

ANDRÉ LAUREN BENJAMIN (AKA ANDRÉ 3000)

Rapper. Actor. Producer. Songwriter.
(May 27, 1975–)

During a 2022 photo shoot, this hip-hop pioneer, half of the Grammy Award–winning duo Outkast, talked about the importance of both artistic creation and self-worth—an awareness that allows one's most authentic self to emerge. That "primal self," as he called it, holds immense power when shared with the world.

"BELIEVE IT. IF YOU BELIEVE IT, THEN IT'LL CARRY YOU."

MYLES FROST

(July 21, 1999–)

Broadway actor. Dancer. Singer.

Myles Frost, the youngest winner of the Tony Award for Best Lead Actor in a Musical, spoke about his approach to preparing for his breakout role as Michael Jackson in the Broadway production *MJ*. He explained in the 2022 interview that he was in his last year of college when he received the phone call to audition, and though he had never acted professionally before, he decided to put his maximum effort into securing the part. Frost's commitment to and belief in a highly unlikely circumstance being uniquely tailored for him helped to ensure him a historical debut and inspires others to believe in their abilities.

"All too often, Black culture is so easily disposable in every aspect. TikTok content creations, our slang, our music, our style. I guess the attitude has always been 'It's not a big deal. It's just a dance; it's just a concert.' But it *is* a big deal."

AHMIR THOMPSON (AKA QUESTLOVE)

DJ. Drummer and bandleader. Producer. Author. Oscar-winning film director. (January 20, 1971–)

Questlove directed a critically acclaimed documentary about the widely unknown 1969 Harlem Cultural Festival, earning himself several prestigious awards, including the coveted Academy Award for Best Documentary Feature. In a 2021 online interview, he referred to himself as "a VHS, Super-8 collecting archivist" and mused about the need to archive Black creativity and culture for historical records and future inspiration.

"I don't think about boundaries.
I don't think about boxes.
I'm an optimist that believes in creativity
and . . . when you do that,
you start drawing all over the paper
and not within the lines."

VIRGIL ABLOH

**Creative director. Fashion designer. Founder and CEO of Off-White.
(September 30, 1980–November 28, 2021)**

In an online discussion about creating for the future, Virgil Abloh encouraged listeners to be eternal optimists who are curious. Those characteristics, he said, paired with thinking outside the box, lead to creative innovation.

"Our journey has never been one of shortcuts or settling for less. It has not been the path for the faint-hearted, for those that prefer leisure over work, or seek only the pleasures of riches and fame. Rather, it has been the risk-takers, the doers, the makers of things—some celebrated, but more often men and women obscure in their labor— who have carried us up the long rugged path towards prosperity and freedom."

BARACK HUSSEIN OBAMA

Forty-fourth president of the United States.
(August 4, 1961–)

In his inaugural address delivered in Washington, DC, on January 20, 2009, President Obama, the first Black man elected to the office of president of the United States, acknowledged that the country was facing many crises, including wars, violence, hatred, a struggling economy, and deep pain; but he also asserted that both individually and collectively, Americans could and would cast pettiness aside and do the necessary work to ensure a better future for all.

"It means something when young African-American kids can go into a museum and see someone who looks like themselves. It gives a sense of 'I belong to the conversation around power—who has it, who's allowed to inherit that dignity.'"

KEHINDE WILEY

Artist.
(February 28, 1977–)

While discussing with TV host Trevor Noah his creative process for painting the official presidential portrait of Barack Obama for the National Portrait Gallery and sculpting his statue entitled *Rumors of War*, Kehinde Wiley explained the significance of Black imagery having a presence in high art, as it confirms to viewers that they are powerful and will remain so for centuries to come.

"SO EARLY IN LIFE, I HAD LEARNED THAT IF YOU WANT SOMETHING, YOU HAD BETTER MAKE SOME NOISE."

MALCOLM X

Human rights activist. Civil rights leader. Muslim minister.
(May 19, 1925–February 21, 1965)

In his 1965 *Autobiography of Malcolm X*, the author and activist shared lessons gleaned from his life experiences and offered insights into how to improve Black American citizens' plight. In this quote, he reflects on how his mother dismissed his older siblings' requests for after-school snacks but would cave to Malcolm when he fussed and complained relentlessly for food. Closed mouths, he learned, don't get fed—a lesson he applied in his activism as an adult.

"I DON'T REALLY CARE SO MUCH
WHAT PEOPLE SAY ABOUT ME
BECAUSE IT USUALLY IS A REFLECTION
OF WHO THEY ARE."

PRINCE ROGERS NELSON

Musician. Singer. Songwriter. Producer.
(June 7, 1958–April 21, 2016)

Prince was asked in a 2004 interview if he concerns himself with what other people think of him. The music icon replied that others' opinions did not matter to him, as they tend to have more to do with those who are vocalizing their ideas, desires, or impressions. This quote illustrates that the most relevant beliefs about self stem from oneself.

> "SOMETIMES YOUR GRADES DON'T GIVE A REAL INDICATION OF WHAT YOUR GREATNESS MIGHT BE."

CHADWICK AARON BOSEMAN

Actor. Humanitarian. Playwright.
(November 29, 1976–August 28, 2020)

While giving the keynote speech at the 150th commencement ceremony of his alma mater, Howard University, the late distinguished actor urged the 2018 graduating class to not only savor achieving a great educational milestone, but also to reflect on the obstacles they overcame while doing so. Boseman explained that while some of the new graduates had faced financial and academic challenges, they should still maintain a deep sense of pride in their accomplishment and know that grades do not always reflect potential for success.

> "FASHION CAN BECOME POLITICAL DEPENDING ON THE WAY YOU SHOW YOUR CLOTHES."

OLIVIER ROUSTEING

Creative director. Fashion designer.
(September 13, 1985–)

This French designer said in a 2019 interview that while there are noteworthy global pushes for women's rights, diversity, inclusivity, and more, many significant social movements can be addressed with and impacted by fashion.

> "I DON'T WRITE FOR A BLACK AUDIENCE. I DON'T WRITE FOR A WHITE AUDIENCE. I WRITE FOR MYSELF."

FREDERICK AUGUST KITTEL JR. (AKA AUGUST WILSON)

Playwright. Author.
(April 27, 1945–October 2, 2005)

Regarded by many as one of the most important African-American playwrights in history, August Wilson focused his work primarily on the Black American lived experience over a span of decades. Because he highlighted Black narratives, attitudes, struggles, and triumphs, many might assume he had a particular audience in mind. However, Wilson's quote serves as an exclamation point on the idea that work done authentically and well to appease one's own satisfaction can have profound societal implications as well.

"I TRAINED MYSELF, YOU KNOW."

JEAN-MICHEL BASQUIAT

Artist.
(December 22, 1960–August 12, 1988)

Basquiat, one of the most prominent and popular artists of neo-Expressionism, shared in a 1985 TV interview that he learned most about art by looking at it and teaching himself. His undeniable success proves that formal study is not the sole path to greatness; it is possible to excel with discipline and self-study.

"THOSE WHO SAY
IT CAN'T BE DONE
ARE USUALLY INTERRUPTED
BY THOSE DOING IT."

JAMES ARTHUR BALDWIN

Activist. Writer.
(August 2, 1924–December 1, 1987)

In his 1955 seminal collection of essays, *Notes of a Native Son*, Baldwin assessed, analyzed, and criticized many aspects of Black American life just as the civil rights movement was finding its footing. While pondering success, the notable writer acknowledged that despite the many setbacks that could deter some from reaching their goals, there are others who find a path to achieving their dreams no matter what obstacles may await them.

"Being able to control your
narrative and tell your story
the way you want to is very important.
The manipulation, the
colonization, the distortion
of stories, narrative, history
has been done forever."

COLIN KAEPERNICK

Activist. Football quarterback. Author. Publisher.
(November 3, 1987–)

Here, the former San Francisco 49ers quarterback, known for kneeling during the American national anthem to protest police brutality and racial inequities in the United States, underscores how important it is for Black people to tell their own stories from their own perspectives—a practice that honors their individual and collective realities, even when others cast their history in a negative light.

"POSSESSIONS MAKE YOU RICH?
I DON'T HAVE THAT TYPE OF RICHNESS.
MY RICHNESS IS LIFE, FOREVER."

ROBERT "BOB" NESTA MARLEY

Singer. Songwriter. Humanitarian.
(February 6, 1945–May 11, 1981)

At the height of Bob Marley's popularity, an interviewer bluntly asked him if he had a lot of money in his bank account. Marley first asked the interviewer what he considered to be a lot of money. When the interviewer suggested millions, Marley countered that while he did not have that amount in his possession, his true wealth came from having eternal life.

> "I BELIEVE IN HOLDING UP A MIRROR TO THE AUDIENCE. I BELIEVE THAT DANCE SHOULD BE EVERY SHAPE, COLOR, AND SIZE, LIKE WE ALL ARE."

ALVIN AILEY JR.

**Choreographer. Dancer. Director. Founder of the Alvin Ailey American Dance Theater.
(January 5, 1931–December 1, 1989)**

When an interviewer asked Alvin Ailey if he searched for a particular body type when casting dancers for his internationally renowned dance company, Ailey insisted that the ballet industry's practice of curating performers according to strict guidelines for body measurements and weight was a tool to keep Black dancers out of premier positions. His 1978 quote articulates his belief that dancers should accurately reflect the diversity of the audience and society.

"THE FIRST CHANGE THAT TAKES PLACE IS IN YOUR MIND. YOU HAVE TO CHANGE YOUR MIND BEFORE YOU CHANGE THE WAY YOU LIVE AND THE WAY YOU MOVE."

GIL SCOTT-HERON

Author. Musician. Poet. Singer.
(April 1, 1949–May 27, 2011)

In one of his most popular songs released in 1971, Gil Scott-Heron boldly proclaimed, "The revolution will not be televised!" When asked to explain what he meant by that phrase, Scott-Heron stated that the catalyst for change would never be captured on film because true change begins from within.

"NOTHING CAN BREAK YOU WHEN YOU HAVE THE SPIRIT."

JOHN LEWIS

**Civil rights activist. Politician. United States representative.
(February 21, 1940–July 17, 2020)**

In his book *Walking with the Wind: A Memoir of the Movement*, Lewis, internationally known as one of the most prominent figures in the American civil rights movement, noted that while struggle was a recurring staple of his life's journey, he felt uniquely prepared to face and surpass any challenges, as the spirit to do so had been passed down to him from his parents, grandparents, and ancestors.

"There are two ways to go through life: as a thermometer or a thermostat. Don't be a thermometer, just reflecting what's around you, going up or down with your surroundings. Be a thermostat and set the temperature."

CORY BOOKER

**Attorney. Author. United States senator.
(April 27, 1969–)**

In his 2016 book, *United: Thoughts on Finding Common Ground and Advancing the Common Good*, Booker provides insights on how we can live our truths in a kind, respectful manner, get active in community work, embrace love over fear, and actively seek purpose in life. In this quote, he's promoting the idea of making intentional life choices and taking the lead in one's own journey.

"Be careful of these people who say, 'You have made it. Take it easy; you don't need any more help.' . . . . Beware of that myth, the myth that everything is going to be all right. Don't give in. . . . Because it seems to me that what we need today is to refocus."

THURGOOD MARSHALL

**Civil rights activist. Lawyer. First African-American justice of the United States Supreme Court.
(July 2, 1908–January 24, 1993)**

In 1978 at the Howard University School of Law, Marshall gave a speech on the subject of equality. The honorable justice warned the audience against becoming complacent in light of the many civil rights victories that had been achieved. He highlights here the importance of maintaining focus on future goals, because even when enormous gains have been made, the work of progress must continue.

> "I SAW THAT THE CAMERA COULD BE A WEAPON AGAINST POVERTY, AGAINST RACISM, AGAINST ALL SORTS OF SOCIAL WRONGS. I KNEW AT THAT POINT I HAD TO HAVE A CAMERA."

GORDON PARKS

Photographer. Director. Writer. Producer.
(November 30, 1912–March 7, 2006)

Widely considered one of the best photographers of his generation, Gordon Parks created images that graced the pages of prominent magazines, museum walls, and even television and movie screens. He captured the very essence of everyday African-American life, showing its beauty, dignity, nuance, and truth, with themes ranging from segregation to luxurious Black living. In this quote, Parks depicts his camera as an unlikely weapon to be wielded against unfair treatment and the stereotyping of Black life.

"YOU'LL NEVER SEE A U-HAUL BEHIND A HEARSE. I DON'T CARE HOW MUCH MONEY YOU MAKE, YOU CAN'T TAKE IT WITH YOU. AND IT'S NOT HOW MUCH YOU HAVE; IT'S WHAT YOU DO WITH WHAT YOU HAVE."

DENZEL WASHINGTON

Actor. Director. Producer.
(December 28, 1954–)

In his 2015 commencement address at Dillard University, this renowned actor imparted life wisdom to the school's graduates, advising them to keep God first, then encouraging them to "fail big" by pushing themselves out of their comfort zones. In this quote, the Academy Award winner recommended focusing on making an impact instead of just an income, as there is no greater reward than the satisfaction of helping others.

> "THE THING IS THAT JUST BECAUSE WE'RE MAGIC DOESN'T MEAN WE'RE NOT REAL."

JESSE WILLIAMS

Actor. Activist. Director. Producer.
(August 5, 1981–)

In his 2016 acceptance speech for the BET Humanitarian Award, Williams delivered an impassioned address reflecting on the dynamics of the many injustices heaped against Blacks in America. He highlighted the need for increased support for Black women, the power of mobilizing as a people, the urgency for police reform, and the strength in spending wealth wisely. He concluded by stating that Black Americans "have been floating this country on credit for centuries," that Black genius has been gentrified, and that "our culture, our dollars, our entertainment" have been extracted like oil. In this quote, Williams aptly reminds listeners that though Black people's natural excellence and gifts often stretch into the realm of what can seem supernatural, their right to exist as real, normal humans remains.

> "YOU CAN'T GET MORE PATRIOTIC THAN SPEAKING TRUTH TO POWER ABOUT WHAT IS WRONG WITH THIS COUNTRY. THAT'S A PATRIOTIC ACT OF THE UTMOST."

SHELTON JACKSON "SPIKE" LEE

(March 20, 1957–)
Actor. Director. Producer. Screenwriter.

In a 2021 *New Yorker* interview, Spike Lee mused on the contributions Black people have made to American society over the years, stating that from the very beginning, Black women and men have been fighting for the United States of America while simultaneously awaiting the fulfillment of the promise of equal rights. He contended that when activists such as Colin Kaepernick use their platforms to point out that that promise is not being delivered—when they call for the ever-present need for change—they are often met with resistance, professional punishment, and ridicule. This quote supports the position that true patriotism is characterized by openly and honestly critiquing the shortcomings of one's country.

> "THE BATTLES THAT COUNT AREN'T THE ONES FOR GOLD MEDALS. THE STRUGGLES WITHIN YOURSELF—THE INVISIBLE, INEVITABLE BATTLES INSIDE ALL OF US—THAT'S WHERE IT'S AT."

JESSE OWENS

Track-and-field athlete. Olympic gold medalist.
(September 12, 1913–March 31, 1980)

In his 1978 memoir, *Jesse: The Man Who Outran Hitler*, the world-renowned sprinter and long jumper reflected on his career achievements as well as his spiritual journey. Having won four gold medals in the 1936 Olympics held in Berlin, Germany, Owens was considered the premier athlete of his time—a living counter to the myth of white supremacy. In this quote, he highlights that the most meaningful victories are not won on a court or a track but are gained when one overcomes personal challenges and struggles to achieve their goals.

"I BELIEVE THAT NOT ONLY CHILDREN,
BUT ADULTS AS WELL,
WE ALL NEED TO KNOW HOW
TO EXPRESS OURSELVES."

SAVION GLOVER

Choreographer. Master tap dancer. Actor.
(November 19, 1973–)

Savion Glover became one of the most internationally recognizable staples in modern dance by mastering theory and technique and by following the lead of such great mentors as Sammy Davis Jr. and Gregory Hines. But Glover says his preferred method of dancing, teaching, and learning is to be in touch with how he is feeling and then to express that emotion through dance. This quote conveys that there are numerous ways to express oneself and that mastering how to do so is a valuable life skill.

> "A LIFE IS NOT IMPORTANT
> EXCEPT IN THE IMPACT
> IT HAS ON OTHER LIVES."

JACKIE ROBINSON

Baseball player.
(January 31, 1919–October 24, 1972)

As the very first African-American man to play Major League Baseball, Jackie Robinson encountered many challenges and setbacks during his groundbreaking career. In his 1972 memoir, *I Never Had It Made*, he reflects on activism, baseball, playing and winning in racist environments, family, perseverance, and resilience. In this quote, the legendary ballplayer asserts that helping others is what makes our existence significant.

"THE GREAT PART ABOUT BEING IN ANY SITUATION, WHETHER YOU'RE UP OR DOWN IN LIFE, IS THAT IT'S AN AMAZING OPPORTUNITY, AND YOU HAVE THE ABILITY TO CHANGE EVERY SITUATION."

SEAN ANDERSON (AKA BIG SEAN)

Rapper.
(March 25, 1988–)

As a guest on a health podcast in 2022, Big Sean discussed his approach to maintaining his mental, physical, and spiritual wellness while achieving high levels of success. The musician underlined the importance of gratitude and meditation in his life, as both have assisted him in viewing obstacles as opportunities for growth. This quote illustrates Big Sean's belief that every moment in life is filled with possibilities and should be appreciated as such.

"SOMETIMES YOU GOT TO REMIND YOURSELF WHY YOU'RE DOING IT, WHAT THE MEDIUM IS CAPABLE OF, AND THAT'LL GIVE ME A LITTLE BIT OF GAS TO KEEP GOING."

RYAN COOGLER

Director. Producer. Screenwriter.
(May 23, 1986–)

In a 2018 roundtable discussion with other filmmakers, Coogler, the acclaimed director of the blockbuster film *Black Panther*, explained that not knowing other directors, paying for expensive film school, and general fatigue from hard work made excelling in his career challenging. To motivate himself, he watched movies that both inspired and reminded him of why he chose to work in film. His quote reminds us that overcoming obstacles in pursuit of our dreams requires us to concentrate on our purpose and the endless possibilities.

"YOU GOTTA BE ABLE TO COMPETE. STEEL SHARPENS STEEL. YOU GOTTA GET OUT THERE AND YOU GOTTA EARN YOUR SPOT. IT'S NOT GIVEN."

SHAWN CARTER (AKA JAY-Z)

Rapper. Entrepreneur. Producer. Record executive.
(December 4, 1969–)

This business mogul and rap icon reminisced in a 2013 radio interview about the seminal body of work he and his contemporaries released around the same time; everyone, he noted, was hugely popular and successful. In this quote, Jay-Z stresses putting forth your best effort and doing the necessary work to achieve your goals, even when the competition is stiff, because taking on the challenge of engaging with the best only makes one better.

"DON'T BE AFRAID OF FAILURE. THIS IS THE WAY TO SUCCEED."

LEBRON JAMES

Professional basketball player. Entrepreneur. School owner.
(December 30, 1984–)

In his 2009 memoir, *Shooting Stars*, Lebron James shares valuable lessons gleaned from his experiences as a young Black man in Akron, Ohio, as well as from his journey to becoming a preeminent player in the National Basketball Association, considered one of the best athletes in the world. James recounts many stories of setbacks in his career and personal life, including being born to a single, teenage mother, facing racial and social injustices, and losing many individual games and championships during his career. While some may view failure as an experience to avoid, this star player believes it's the path to success.

BELIEVE IN

BLACK MEN